FOREWORD

GW00950040

For an introduction to this book, I was
to me, love has so many different interpretations. Its definition is but
everybody's own!

But thus, it might be important, for one to understand my interpretation of love
and this book.

My poems come straight from the heart, and poetry to me, is another language.
For a long time, after all, it was the only way I felt I could express myself fully.
It's the only way I understand and understood, myself.

So, this book is all about love.

How it hurts, how it heals, how it scars, how it makes you not want to continue
living any longer. Because oh how it can hurt! But to me, it makes living life
worth it.

Love, after all, is one of the most pure and natural of feelings. It lives within you,
within me and within the animal kingdom.

So feel it, express it, at any moment you can, as I promise you, you will never
regret it!

My advice to whoever reads this is: love, and love, and love some more. From
the heart, ruthlessly, unforgivingly, endlessly and completely. Be genuine in
your love, and honest and don't expect anything in return. It is liberating, it is
freeing, it is love. It is one of the greatest, if not THE greatest, gifts you can
give yourself, and others.

With love,
Tuuli

They say, we are at war with ourselves

Love thyself first,
Is this just a motto,
or a way of life?
Is this how I win the lotto?
And finally sleep at peace with myself.

It's true, I used to think about this often.
My hatred of myself and towards myself,
got in the way often.

I think, to hate yourself first,
leads towards a pathway to love.
Love and acceptance,
to my honest truth,
complete acceptance.

I know my mistakes,
I know my flaws.
Yes there are aplenty,
but to forgive yourself first,
is to accept yourself.
Accept life and the path I am on,
no matter how broken,
no matter how wrong,
No matter how long.

Speak truth to your freedom,
even if a whisper,
even if a song,
I accept myself and my life as they are,
I have become strong.
Strong for me,

Strong for us,
Strong for you,
Strong for life.
We move on.

Love

So disorientating, so cruel on the heart.
So sweet,
I say as I drink poison from your lips.
Purple, freezing lips,
I defrost, instantly.
My heart cold, almost frozen over,
until you come in,
into my life,
Again, and all over again.
If hell hath frozen over,
I'd cross it.
For your lips.
Sweet like sugar,
Perfectly fine.
My fury relinquishes its control,
of hurt passed,
of control of my emotions,
of my love, my care.
Defrost me all you will,
trust you I will!
Forever I will!
Just choose me!
And dedicate your whole full self,
to Me.
I know it's asking for much,

as there's another 7 billion hearts to crush.

Choose me,

Please.

You must.

Your bloodstream

Do you know what it feels like,
when you give me none of your time?

My heart's been trampled on,
time and time again;
Every day I suffer,
give me a second of your oxygen,
and I fall,
I fall,
I'm falling.
Back in love,
I fall again.

A second of your time,
is all I am needing.
Is all I am asking for.
Why torture me, like this?
Do you not see my eyes?
Do you not realize?
There's blood dripping from my incisors.
A millimeter at a time,
it drains your shirt,
your eyes,
your blood.
We're intertwined.

Slowly,
I enter your soul,
pull on your heart,
the strings tougher than my might.
I keep pulling,
pulling,

pulling until I fall apart.
We're untangled again.
I'm crying.
Not even a second of your oxygen,
did you think was worth your time.

I will be half,
or less.
Bloodied,
at best.

Unrequited, again

My heart so fully strung.
You tell me no words.
I, obviously,
deserve none.

So I sit here awake,
again, and again,
and again.

I fiddle my thumbs,
I scratch my head,
I drink until I drown.
I pull out my hair.
Drink again, everything, including acid.

If you give me no emotions,
I shall find my own,
from sources already well-known to me:
acid,
grass,
pins & needles,
a troll's cry.
I am the troll,
as I beg for something I should not.

Patience is not a virtue,
not to me.
I sit here,
patiently.
Yes.
And it eats, slowly, at my heart.
I am bleeding,

again.
Not sleeping,
again.
Your acid love is burning,
again.
And I let it,
once again.

What a fool is this woman?
Her heart open to anyone,
anything,
as she thinks it makes her feel alive.
But the truth is?
The truth is?
She's been asleep for a while,
unconscious but subconsciously operating,
Every move like a scripture in a book.
A bible, perhaps,
just not as holy,
Nothing like that.

She just moves,
and destroys herself,
looking for love,
his love,
just his.
So she destroys herself.

Love through all its hazy lines

I love how you lied.
I love how what you defined to be me;
was a lie.

You went through life,
like a hurricane of death,
collecting vials of blood.

Yes, I did collapse at your feet,
begging for your time.
At that moment, I was but desperate,
I was young,
I almost died.
I thought you were deserving of my love,
my kindness,
my time.

You sunk your teeth into my neck,
my life,
my veins,
my time.

I gave you all my love.
It wasn't enough.
So soon enough,
I withdrew myself,
and went on an emotional prowl.
Anybody to give me their ear,
their arms,
any limb!
Anything!
But mostly their time.

I was desperate,
I cried.
I hugged.
I filed a motion of begging,
of anything,
anywhere,
any time.

Of course you didn't know;
as you simply continued your massacre.
Of every heart,
emotion,
mind.

You didn't care for the destruction,
of any restriction,
of hearts broken.
You just sought your next vile of blood.

Any victory was good enough.
As my soul slowly died.
I withdrew from myself,
as I sought to understand your method,
your anger,
your lies.
I was dumb.
I should have killed you,
and died.
And saved my time.

Dear

My darling.
Your edges so beautiful.
Your smile makes me smile.
Your attention makes me long for more.
Your care makes me fall.
Further and further in.
In love.
I hate to admit it,
because let's face it,
I've been hurt before.
Scarred.
Stabbed in the heart to say the least.
But at least,
I still believe in this.
Still.
I commit to you,
regardless of everything.
I've seen you in my dreams.
Yes, that's what my dreams are made of.
I see you.
You love me.
Completely,
regardlessly,
unconditionally.
I wish I could have you now,
forever,
and ever.
And forever more.

The one that got away

You don't get it.
And honestly? I'm not expecting you to.
But when I sit here, and tears have carved pathways down my eyes.
I do wonder why.
Why don't you get it?
Why don't you wonder why?
Why I cry?
Why my sadness stretches for miles.
Why she cries?
But I'll go on living.
God knows I will try.
But don't go sitting by my river,
too late,
and asking why?

Boundless

My insanity needs no box.
If boxed, it would seep out,
and leave you perplexed.

Why is she like this?
What is she doing?
What is she thinking?

My heart's not for the sinker man.
I float forever, in space, notwithstanding gravity.
Don't bound my soul,
my desires,
my thoughts,
my heart.

I will break free, eventually,
and I know that's something you can't see.
So you try and control my heart,
my thoughts,
my soul,
temporarily.
Until I erupt, and relight my fire.
Until I erupt and you're no longer the one I desire.

Perfect?

Ever the perfectionist.
I hate every word I write,
what was I thinking?
This doesn't sound right.
To love is to define it yourself.
Every soul for themselves.
Who am I to dictate anything?
Even to grace a piece of paper with the word.
As if I know!
My heart's been broken.
and I still think it's gold.
Ludicrous!
Absolutely insane!
But have you felt it?
Have you seen it?
Can You define it?
It's hard.
Impossible to say.
It's that feeling, you know!
It's that feeling I say.
The feeling that makes you feel like everything,
well, it might just be okay.
Oh but to love.
That I know.
I have plenty to give.
To anyone!
You!
And you too!
Just love me,
whichever way you define it,
love me the way you know how.
Just love me,

and I'll respond, the only way I know how.

Welcome, welcome

Attention, attention,
I only want more.
Who the hell am I?
But a little whore.
Welcome to your show,
let the game begin.
It starts now.

Continued to the show is your mister,
and milady.
One crazy,
the other crazy about himself, baby.

She looks at him, he looks at her,
apathetically at best.
Musings are very few to go around,
in his head.

She trips over, she shaves her head.
She drowns her sorrows,
but sheds very little tears.

Out of the window he looks,
still apathetic, perhaps even half dead,
his heart on the other side of the world.

But the girl dances and dances,
she goes fast and then extremely slow.
Her feet are bleeding,
her heart slowly shrinking.

The protagonist more than half dead,

drops himself out of the window.
Almost fully dead.

He realizes that in his musings,
the haze of love,
the love of his life was not half way over,
she was right there.
Now herself,
half dead.

Bleeding feet, bleeding heart,
and completely ruthless.
She stabs him in the heart,
with moments of her life to spare.

So there they both lie,
the unrequited and the protagonist,
both dead.

Holy Grail

Don't make me hurt you.
Don't make me do it.
Because you know who does it well?
You know who leaves no trace?
I'd hurt you, if I could,
but the effort is more deserving than you.

So I lay my hands to rest,
peacefully by my side.
I lay my heart at ease,
and whisper into the clouds instead,
I cry.

You lied.
I wish your eyelashes got plucked by a dementor,
I wish your soul got crushed by the demons,
I wish you'd see there's nothing of me that's left in you.

I wish you'd get over your pride, your ego,
and live divine.
But this is your choice,
not mine.

I wish I could lay my head to rest,
my whole spine,
my whole heart,
my whole life.

But I care too much,
for nothing that deserves caring for.
That others would just dump in the gutter;
of your guts,

and core.

But here I sit, quietly contemplating.
Why was this my mistake?
Why did I not just dodge it?
Everybody else seems to know how to!
Everybody else has the answers.
But no,
I, I, I fail,
and pardon my tears at the Holy Grail.

You

The tranquility of your soul leaves me at peace,
puts my mind at ease,
brings you closer to me.

Your touches like rose petals on my skin.
They touch more of my heart than ever my skin;

Your thoughts leave me breathless,
I completely give in.
I was lost, only to be found again.

A hundred or a thousand?

Why does it feel like it's been a hundred years already?
The mind seems to work in funny ways.
Overstimulation is no joke,
but still, I draw clowns.

Is the joke on me?
If so, tell me?
Before I die,
all alone.

Ideals

Read me books.
Whisper through every page,
until I fall asleep.

Quietly say, how much you love me,
when I have no idea.
Surprise me,
oh how I hate it,
but surprise me.

Walk with me in the rain,
and wipe away my tears.
Don't mind my sadness,
or my fears.

Live, live, live, through me,
beside me,
with me,
and promise me forever.

Life

Every scar on my body has been earned.
Toiled for.
Cried for.
Blessed.

You're so certain,
that my scars show flaws.
Show mistakes.
Show no growth.

I think the opposite,
as I see myself,
from within.
Through the guts,
throughout the pins.

I don't lie,
I don't sin.
The scars came from,
whatever was.
Whatever needed to change me.
Not just from within.
I changed, whilst you sinned.
I changed both on the outside,
and within.

To hell with your opinions,
this is only where I begin.

Love

How to define it.
How to speak of it.
How to display it.

I knew it was it.
It took me,
my breath,
my consciousness,
my all.

I forgot everything.
I forgot my flaws,
and yours.
Just to see you,
just to feel you,
just to breathe the air you breathe,
together.

It took me by surprise.
But at the same time I knew.
You were mine,
and I was yours.
Or were you just mine only?
Funny how it didn't matter.
Your eyes were mine only,
even if only for a moment,
but they were mine only.

Oh how I loved you,
oh how I was falling.
Oh how I was,
in love.

Friends & enemies

One time, two times,
one trick pony.
Fool me once,
never again.

It's not as if anyone is below me,
but throw me in the junk and you get to know,
who I can be.
Who I can become.

Scoopidy scoop scoop.
Who gets the next swirl;
and gets thrown right out of the soup?

Friends, or enemies, foes or just the ones I decided to keep?

One time, two times.
No, one time only.
Fool me once and thrown out you shall be.

There are no friends once they become your enemies.

At night

Do you notice, how I type at night?
While my baby's asleep,
the tears roll bitterly from my eyes.

Do you notice how I miss you, when it's night?
You see the truth, but not in full,
my care and attention is never not full.

When I run upstairs,
as my baby's had a fright,
I still think of you.

I think of you, most, at night.
And sometimes I feel guilty,
maybe some think I just might, maybe I should.
I don't care, it's my life.

But what would you do when it seems wrong,
but makes you feel so right?
I have rights.
I deserve these nights.
When I can think of you, uninterrupted,
and dedicate myself, just to you.

Sick

Sickened to the core,
I burn rubbish that you tore.
Tore at me,
to get to me.
Push all them buttons.

You're pissing at my life, or,
yours instead.
It's easy to flee, isn't it?
Relinquish all responsibilities.

Leave this, leave that,
leave holes poked in everybody's head.

You're an asshole in the shed.
Hiding,
always hiding.
Hiding your head,
as your soul does not exist.

Flower, flower

Plucking petals off my flower,
myself.
Getting rid of the ones that don't fulfil their promise;
whose colour is matted and tired;
whose purpose is worn out and expired.

A drop of happiness is all that will qualify,
who will stay,
and who will not.

Petal, petal, petal,
thank you for the memories,
thank you for your time.
Goodbye.

Catch me if you can

A hundred miles I run away.
I run, and I run.
But what if there's no escape?

What if, what if,
you find me.
Cage me.
Feed me lies,
and betray me.
Again, all over.
Flipped over backwards,
I bend over.

Once again, I give up on myself.
I change, as you take control.
Of my thoughts, my actions,
the not so quiet wickedness of my soul.
That keeps me alive,
keeps Me in control.

What if I succumb again?
To the need for love,
to the need of acceptance.
To the softness of your embrace;

I don't want to fail,
again.
Stop me.
But don't catch me if you can.

Victorious

Jury's adjourned.
You're off the hook again.
Again;
Again:
again.

I am stronger now but why is it that you always seem to win?
Every time.

The jury's adjourned again.
They let you off but don't worry I will begin,
and start all over,
again.

Justice prevails in all matters sinister.
Justice in the heart,
Justice in the soul,
Justice on your day in court.

The tables will turn,
and I will win.

Oh your mind

You know I find the mind so hot.
Hit me with that knowledge and I,
and I, well I, I'm shot.

Dead, but so alive.
Wanting more,
I lean at your feet,
I cry.

Always available to your elixir.
Never asleep, always awake.
Waiting for a moment.
Any moment!
Any time!
Any inkling of your time.

Give me life!
Give me your time.
I don't normally beg,
but for that, I would try!

Me

Oh but do I bother you?
With my secret spillings?

Oh but why does my quietness leave you stirred?
My words, after all, don't hurt you.
And this predicament is nothing you are in.

So why be so unkind?
Let my words unwind and pet your ears.
Sweet nothingness is what I need to release.
Do you care?

You

I devour in your humour.
After all, your tongues are but a few.
Honoured to be in your presence,
your wit surely sweeps me off my feet.

I mean, the looks can't be discarded,
albeit secondary.
But my gosh, how to melt butter!
Yes, the butter is I!
How I melt whilst I look into the sky,
my wish is but many,
just one,
just you.

Release

Take, take, take, take, just bloody take already!
Keep taking, keep taking...
I know you never have enough,
until I say, enough!
So just keep on taking.

You'll never understand the depths of my heart,
let alone my soul.
So on the surface,
yes the surface,
only the surface shall I keep on giving.
Fake like a mothertucker, as I cry myself to bed.
Fake like a motherfucker,
I equate your love to nothing.

Oh for thy scum to smell so good

Oh for thy soul to be so crippled,
and so weak.

Courage lacking, you peek,
your steps still creak.
But still you step closer.

Your cowardice leaves you without coverage,
your soul leaves you wide open.
Your smile smells like scum.
I need another cup of rum.
Yeah a cup I say;
whilst a whole bottle sways my way.

This momentary weakness gives you no victory.
Oh don't think that, for a second.
Your consciousness still lies in the ditch.
Fuck you and that bitch.

Broken

Whilst I am angry, confused, heartbroken,
I write this message.
I feel broken.

Take another leaf out of my book,
at least burn it.
Don't leave it broken.

Clarity would help,
so would a drop of comradery and friendship.
But I can't mask this feeling.
So I deny myself all of it.

Perhaps to live through every inch of this moment,
means,
I will live again.
Maybe even feel alive again!

Family

You know when they talk about family.
Real family.
A bond stronger than Italian blood.
Do you know who they talk about?
Do you know what they talk about?

Wow.

If I could tell you.
My family.
They talk about mine.

Wow.

My cornerstone.
My rocks.
The cement of my existence.

Wow.

They are mine.
I am blessed,
for they are mine;
and I can call them my own.
Forever.
They are mine.

My daughter

My life, my life, my life.
All my power, all my might.

Sometimes,
I do not think I am up for this fight.
Weak, weakness, weakness,
it trickles through.

But my life, my life, my life,
you give me strength.
You wipe away my tears,
You give me all my might.

You're a bigger support to me,
than you'll ever know!

You hug my tears into laughter.
You give me all of your time.

My tiny rock,
my diamond in disguise of a child.

You are my life, my life,
my everything.
My daughter.
My fight.
My life.

Sugar beans

Failing to see daylight,
I call for the sun.
Dreams are made out of sugar beans,
I trigger my gun.

Failing to see daylight,
I pray for the moon.
I call for everything,
That I know to be good.

The moon would not answer my prayers.
So I went and cried by the grave of a slave,
and he told me: "All you can do, is be brave";

Now, again, I trigger my gun.
And shoot down the moon.
Pull down the sun,
and plant it near my sugar beans.

My dreams will soon come,
and they will come true.

I whisper to myself,
and I am fast asleep by my dear sugar beans.

Are you there?

Love me in whatever way.
I pray, I pray,
the only way,
I know how.

Suddenly, you're gone.
I pray, I pray, the only way it matters.

Love might be the only way,
so I'll love you more to compensate.
Destitute, in silence,
locked away in surrender.

I give you all, in silence.
Internally at peace, dedicated and committed.

I pray more, louder, more in your name,
more, more and I give again.

Surrendered to you I have, fully.
Truly yours, so deeply.

Do you hear my prayer?
Do you not hear my silent cry?
Should I do more?
I have died inside.

I can't any more!
I pray for you to pray for me instead,
as I am dead inside.

Only fulfilled by unrequited dreams,

so lost, and again,
I start again.

Empty

Void, so void,
I slip venom in your brain.
Slip in my fangs and I take the reins.

I envy your thoughts and your pain.
Let me see what it's like to feel again.

Teach me, obey me, drive me insane!
Give me an inch of what I am to gain.

I still don't feel it, so I go deeper again.
I know it mortifies you when I go insane,
but let me play my game.

You know it's for us, right?
Manipulation, after all, exists at every turn.
Let's not deny it and honey,
let's feel the burn.

I don't know if it hurts,
I am numb to this curse.
I feel nothing, nothing,
so is it you it hurts?

I know I've been cursed, as I want it to hurt!
I want to think, feel, suffer and feel the same.

I'm alive, only barely,
with my name on your lips.
My thoughts illicit,
and my care left for so little.

Printed in Poland
by Amazon Fulfillment
Poland Sp. z o.o., Wrocław

51069063R00026